Marvellous Mix-Ups

Also by Alexander McCall Smith

Marvellous Mix-Ups

ALEXANDER McCALL SMITH

Illustrated by
Kate Hindley

BLOOMSBURY
LONDON OXFORD NEW YORK NEW DELHI SYDNEY

Bloomsbury Publishing, London, Oxford, New York, New Delhi and Sydney

The Spaghetti Tangle first published in Great Britain in 1991
by Methuen Children's Books
Teacher Trouble first published in Great Britain in 1994
by Young Corgi Books

This edition published in September 2016 by Bloomsbury Publishing Plc
50 Bedford Square, London WC1B 3DP

www.bloomsbury.com

BLOOMSBURY is a registered trademark of Bloomsbury Publishing Plc

A CIP catalogue record for this book is available from the British Library

ISBN 978 1 4088 6588 0

Typeset by RefineCatch Limited, Bungay, Suffolk

Printed and bound in Great Britain by CPI Group (UK) Ltd, Croydon CR0 4YY

1 3 5 7 9 10 8 6 4 2

For Tsoona Drew Copping

THE SPAGHETTI TANGLE

~ 1 ~
Aunt Rebecca

There were once two children who had never eaten spaghetti. John and his sister Nicky would have loved to have eaten spaghetti, but they were never allowed to do so much as taste it because of Aunt Rebecca.

John and Nicky had lived with their aunt for as long as they could remember. Their parents were experts on volcanoes, which is about one of the most dangerous jobs there is. They had to live in far-off places, waiting for volcanoes to erupt so that they could tell people what to do about it. It was far too dangerous a life for children and they had reluctantly had to pass John and Nicky over to Aunt Rebecca.

Aunt Rebecca was a kind-hearted person, in a funny sort of way, and the children were fond of her – also in a funny sort of way. They knew that, for some reason, she was not very happy with life but they had never been able to work out exactly why this was.

"I think she's grumpy because the person she wanted to marry her never did so," said Nicky one day when Aunt Rebecca had been particularly grouchy.

Their aunt had once told the children that she had been engaged to be married to somebody but that the wedding had been called off at the last moment. But she had not said more than that, and the whole thing remained a bit of a mystery.

Life with Aunt Rebecca was a little bit strange. It was not that she was always grumpy – she wasn't. But when she wasn't grumpy, she would almost certainly do rather odd things. For instance, they might find Aunt Rebecca in the sitting room, dancing to music. And it was not the sort of dancing that you might do by yourself, it was as if she was pretending to be dancing with somebody. She would have her arms held out before her, a dreamy look on her face, and she would whirl about the room just as if she were being guided by an invisible partner. This meant that the children were worried about bringing friends back to the house – just in case something embarrassing happened. And for this reason, they had fewer friends than other people. But they were fond enough of one another's company and they saw their friends at school.

Aunt Rebecca also had firm ideas about a number of things, and the most important of these matters was food.

"People eat the most dreadful rubbish," she would say. "Look at all that terrible butter and sugar and other unhealthy things they put down their throats!"

Aunt Rebecca's idea of a healthy meal was carrot soup followed by raw cabbage and nuts and washed down with tomato juice. Now this was all very healthy, of course, and tasty too, but if you ate nothing else, then you began to want something different.

"Oh, for some chips!" John whispered to his sister as they sat down to their raw onion rings and diced turnip.

"I'd give anything for a piece of chocolate cake!" replied Nicky under her breath. "With a twirl of cream on the top!"

"What was that!" barked Aunt Rebecca, looking sternly at the children. "Did you say something about the onions?"

"No, Aunt," said John in a sad voice. "We said nothing about onions."

"A fine vegetable, the onion," said Aunt Rebecca, peering at the pile of raw onion on her plate. "It's very good for the blood, you know."

"And they make you smell," Nicky murmured.

"What?" snapped Aunt Rebecca. "What was that?"

"I said, 'And they keep you well'," said Nicky timidly.

"Indeed they do," said Aunt Rebecca. "Now eat up, children. There's a nice glass of carrot juice to follow."

It was difficult for the children not to think about food. Every day, on their way home from school, they would pass the doors of the best restaurant in town. And every time they went past, their noses would catch the delicious cooking smells.

The children would have loved to eat in the restaurant, but how could they? Then, one Friday, Nicky had an extraordinary stroke of luck.

She had received a letter that morning from an uncle, who lived far away, but

who always sent birthday presents. This year he had forgotten to do so and had written to tell her how sorry he was. And in the letter, to make up for the birthday present, he sent Nicky a crisp new banknote. Nicky had never had so much money before and she found it difficult to make up her mind as to what to do with it.

"You could buy a new pen," John suggested, as they walked home from school together.

"I've got a pen," Nicky said.

"Or you could buy a game," John went on.

"I don't want one," said Nicky.

They were now just outside the restaurant. From within, there came the delicious smell of cooking, and they both stopped to sniff the air.

"I could take us to lunch," Nicky said suddenly, her face breaking into a smile.

"Do you really want to?" John said, hardly daring believe the offer.

"Yes," said Nicky, firmly. "Let's go straight in."

And they did.

~ 2 ~
A Delicious Discovery

"**A** table for two, please," said Nicky to the waiter as he glided forward to meet them.

"Of course," said the waiter politely. "Would you please come with me."

They followed him to a table near the

window. There he drew out the chairs and invited them to sit down. Laid out on the table there was a crisp white tablecloth, shining silver knives and forks, and sparkling crystal glasses.

With a flourish the waiter produced the menu.

"I shall be back soon," he said. "I shall take your order then."

Nicky opened the menu and looked at the list of dishes it contained. Many of them were written in French, and she had no idea what they were. Others were easier to understand. She knew what roast beef was and she had a good idea what chocolate meringue would look like. Then her face fell. John noticed. "What's wrong?" he asked.

"I've just seen what it all costs," Nicky whispered. "I haven't got nearly enough money."

She passed the menu over to her brother. He turned pale as he read.

"There's nothing here that we can afford," he said. "We'll have to sneak out."

They looked about them. Their table was far from the door and they would have to walk past everybody else if they were to leave.

"Come on," said John, beginning to push his chair back. "There's no point in staying."

At that moment, the swing doors into the kitchen opened and out came the waiter. Smiling, he crossed the restaurant to stand at the side of their table.

"Well," he said cheerfully. "Have you had the time to make your choice?"

Nicky gazed down at the tablecloth.

"I'm sorry," she said, in a small voice. "We haven't got enough money. It all costs far too much."

John braced himself for the waiter's anger.

The waiter said nothing for a few moments. Then, he leant forward, and whispered, "How much have you got? You show me."

Nicky took the note out of her pocket and showed it to him.

"Oh dear," said the waiter. "I can see that you have no idea how much restaurants cost." He shook his head. "Oh dear! Oh dear!"

"Don't worry," said John. "We'll go right now. And we're sorry for wasting your time."

"Oh no you don't," the waiter said. "It's a rule at any really good restaurant that nobody goes out hungry. You were my guests the moment you stepped in the door, and I won't have my guests disappointed."

"Do you really mean that?" asked Nicky.

"Of course I do," said the waiter. "Now, what I suggest is that we think of something that doesn't cost quite as much as the dishes on the menu. I'll get the chef to make it specially for you."

The waiter thought for a moment, then he made his suggestion.

"I know!" he said. "What about a good bowl of spaghetti? You could afford that."

Nicky looked at John, who said nothing.

"Well," said the waiter. "You like spaghetti, don't you?"

"No," said Nicky. "I mean yes. I mean, well, we've never actually eaten spaghetti."

The waiter straightened up in astonishment.

"You've never eaten spaghetti!" he exclaimed. "Do you mean to say you've never even tasted it?"

"No," said Nicky. "We've never even tasted it. You see, we live with our aunt, and she's the President of the Carrot and Nut League, and . . ."

The waiter cut her short.

"Let's waste no more time," he said. "Two spaghettis coming up!"

John and Nicky did not have to wait long. Within minutes, the waiter had placed before them two large plates of spaghetti, topped with generous

helpings of thick sauce. The mere smell of the mouth-watering dish was almost enough for the children; but the taste, and the feel, and the longness of it . . . well, there are no words lengthy enough to describe all that.

At the end of the meal, with their plates scraped quite clean, Nicky paid and the two of them said goodbye to the waiter.

"Come back one day," the waiter said, with a smile.

Nicky nodded, but she knew that there was very little chance that they would be able to afford another meal. And as for John, he knew that it would be a long, long time, if ever, before they tasted spaghetti again.

~ 3 ~
A Very Special Competition

I t was back to carrot juice and raw onion again, with only the memory of that delicious spaghetti to keep them going. They tried to raise the subject of spaghetti with Aunt Rebecca, but it merely sent her into a rage.

"Certainly not!" she exploded. "I'm not having that stuff in my kitchen. The mere thought of it!"

"But there's nothing wrong with spaghetti," John pleaded. "It's quite healthy."

"But look what people put on it," Aunt Rebecca replied heatedly. "Thick red sauce, full of Heaven knows what! Oils, spices, grease, meat, and so on. No. Absolutely not."

John gave up, and Nicky didn't even bother to argue with her aunt.

"One day," she said to herself. "One day I shall have spaghetti again. I know I shall!"

Several weeks later, John was reading a magazine when something caught his eye. There on the page was a brightly-coloured advertisement with a picture of a large bowl of spaghetti. The sight of the spaghetti made his mouth water as it brought back the memory of that marvellous meal in the restaurant. Then he read on, and he realised that here was their chance.

"Look," he said to Nicky. "We shall have to enter."

Nicky took the advertisement and read it through. It had been inserted in the magazine by the manufacturers of Pipelli's Spaghetti, and this is what it said:

Spaghetti is best served with sauce, as we all know. But what sauce is best? Everybody has his or her favourite, so why not send us your recipe? We shall choose the one we think is best, and as a prize the winner will be invited to lunch with our chairman, Mr Pipelli, right here in our spaghetti works. You will see how spaghetti is made and you will even be able to try your hand at making some yourself! So enter straight away!

Nicky glanced at John.

"Do you really think we could enter?" she said. "Do you think we'd stand a chance?"

"Of course we would," replied John. "Somebody's got to win."

"But what about a recipe?" asked Nicky. "I don't have a recipe for sauce."

"I've already thought about that," John said. "Do you remember that sauce we had at the restaurant? Well, we could ask the chef if he would give us the recipe and if we could use it for the competition. It doesn't have to be your own invention – it only has to be your favourite recipe."

Nicky was doubtful, but when John promised that he would do the asking at the restaurant, she agreed. Cutting the entry form out of the magazine, she tucked it into her pocket.

"What are you doing?" Aunt Rebecca asked sharply, but before Nicky could reply a pan of parsnips started to boil over in the kitchen and Aunt Rebecca had to dash off to deal with it.

"I can't wait," John whispered. "I've got a feeling that we're going to win."

They went to the restaurant the next day. The waiter recognised them and gave them a warm smile of welcome.

"We're not here to have lunch," said John. "We're here for a recipe."

The waiter was surprised, but when they explained what they had in mind he gave them a wink and told them to wait. A few minutes later, he came out of the kitchen with a piece of paper in his hand.

"The chef didn't mind at all," he said. "In fact, he was flattered by your request. Here's the recipe."

Nicky took the recipe and studied it. Then they both thanked the waiter and left the restaurant.

"I hope you win," he called out. "And the chef hopes so too. He was very interested in the competition and he says that he will enter one of his other recipes as well. But don't worry – he's sure you've got the best one of all!"

~ 4 ~
Waiting to Win

Nicky filled in the form and sent it off to the Pipelli Spaghetti Company. Then the waiting began. The advertisement had said that the results would be announced "within three weeks", and to make sure that they didn't miss the announcement, the children pored over the newspaper every day. And every day they were disappointed.

"I don't know why you're suddenly so interested in the news," Aunt Rebecca said. "I'm sure you must be up to no good."

Then, one Friday afternoon, John saw the item he had been waiting for. It was a small notice, tucked away in the corner of a page. "The results of the Pipelli Spaghetti Competition will be published tomorrow," it said. "Make sure you don't miss them!"

John and Nicky could barely wait. When at last they saw the next day's newspaper, they opened it with shaking hands. Sure enough, there on the front page was a large advertisement headed: Lucky Winner.

"I can't bear to read it," Nicky said. "I'll close my eyes. You read it and tell me if we've won."

Nicky closed her eyes. There was a silence.

"Have we won?" she asked. "Do tell me."

She opened her eyes. John was staring glumly at the page.

"No," he said. "Somebody else won."

He paused. Then, turning sadly to Nicky, he read out what was written in the paper:

There were hundreds and hundreds of entries in the spaghetti competition. Most of the recipes were very good indeed, although some were not. (Some were very bad.) At last the winner has been chosen and a letter has been sent to the fortunate person.

Nicky looked thoughtful. "But it could have been us," she said. "It doesn't say we didn't win. The letter could be on its way to us."

John pondered what his sister said. She could be right. Perhaps there was a letter in the post for them. Perhaps it would arrive tomorrow, or the day after that.

So the next day they waited for the post to drop through the door. Rushing to pick it up, they quickly shuffled through the letters to see if there was anything for them. No. There were one or two bills, a magazine, and several letters from members of the Carrot and Nut League – nothing for them.

It was the same the following day, and the day after that.

"How long do letters take to arrive?" Nicky asked.

"I'm not sure," replied John. "Two or three days. Maybe more."

He knew, though, that there was now no chance of their having won, and when nothing arrived through the post the next day he told Nicky that there was no point in believing any longer that they might have won.

It was bitterly disappointing. They had known that there would have been hundreds of people entering in the competition, and they had known in their heart of hearts that it was very difficult to win a competition like that, and yet it seemed to them as if they might have come so very close.

"Never mind," said John, trying to sound more cheerful. "Whoever did win will be very pleased with the news."

And after that, they did not talk about

the competition any more. They also tried to forget about spaghetti, and to give up all thought of eating it again and they tried to avoid the restaurant. They now crossed the street before they reached it, so that they would not be forced to breathe in the delicious smells or see the diners at their tables. Then, a few days later, as they were walking past on the other side of the street, they heard a shout.

"Hello there!" cried a voice. "Hello, you two!"

John spun round. There, standing in the door of the restaurant and beckoning them across the street, was their friend the waiter.

"I want to speak to you," he shouted
out.

Reluctantly, John and Nicky crossed
the street to stand before the waiter.

"Where have you been?" he asked. "I've been on the look-out for you."

"We've been going home a different way," explained John, without going on to tell him why this was.

"I see," said the waiter. "Anyway, the important thing is that I've found you."

The waiter drew them into the doorway.

"I've got amazing news for you," he confided. "The chef won the spaghetti competition. Isn't that wonderful?"

John glanced at Nicky. So the chef was the lucky person after all. If only he had given them his recipe and kept theirs!

"And you're pleased?" asked the waiter.

"Of course," said John bravely. "Please tell him we're very happy for him."

The waiter laughed. "Happy for yourself, more likely. He can't go."

John and Nicky looked puzzled.

"He can't visit the spaghetti factory," said the waiter. "He's far too busy. And so he wants you two to have his prize for him. He's been in touch with Mr Pipelli, who says that that's perfectly all right with him. All that you have to do is to arrange a time."

John clapped his hands together with delight. He could scarcely believe their good luck. They had resigned themselves to losing the competition, and now it was just as if they had won. He was already beginning to imagine what the factory would be like and what he would say to Mr Pipelli. And Nicky, although still astonished by their sudden stroke of good fortune, was thinking exactly the same thing.

~ 5 ~
A Welcome from Mr Pipelli

Aunt Rebecca was not at all pleased.

"A spaghetti factory!" she exploded. "Did you say a SPAGHETTI factory?"

"Yes," said John. "Mr Pipelli's Spaghetti Factory."

"You can't go," she said. "I won't hear of it."

"But why not?" Nicky pleaded. "There's nothing wrong with spaghetti."

"We've already discussed that," said Aunt Rebecca. "And you know my views. No. And that's all there is to it."

John thought quickly.

"It is rude to turn down an invitation, isn't it?" he asked. He knew very well Aunt Rebecca was most particular about manners.

"Of course it is," snapped his aunt. "It's very rude, unless you've got a good reason."

"Well," said John. "Mr Pipelli has

invited us to have lunch with him in his factory. Surely it would be rude to say no."

Aunt Rebecca was cornered. Eventually, after a lot more grumbling, she had to accept that it would be impolite for John and Nicky not to go, and permission was given.

"Well done!" Nicky whispered to her brother. "I can almost smell the spaghetti already!"

"What was that?" asked Aunt Rebecca suspiciously. "What did you say?"

But, from the kitchen, there came a squeak from the pressure cooker, and Aunt Rebecca had to dash off to attend to a pot of fresh seaweed, which was now done just to a turn.

On the day of the visit, John and Nicky were ready well before the spaghetti factory car arrived. The driver settled them in their seats, and they began the long journey to the factory.

"You'll like Mr Pipelli," the driver said. "Everybody likes him the moment they meet him. You just wait and see."

They drove for an hour or so before they arrived. It was a very large factory – much bigger than either of them had imagined – and over the front gate there was a great sign made out of metal letters:

PIPELLI'S SPAGHETTI – THE KING OF SPAGHETTIS.

The car swept into the driveway and came to a halt outside the main office. Ushered into the entrance hall by the driver, the two visitors were shown to a door which said, quite simply, THE BOSS.

"Go on," said the driver. "Knock."

And Nicky did.

The door flew open the moment Nicky's knuckle hit the wood. There, before them, stood a stout man in a checked suit. He had curly black hair, sparkling eyes and a smile that seemed to split his face in two.

"Well, well," he said. "My two guests! Please come in!"

John and Nicky entered the room cautiously. It was a more splendid office than they had ever imagined. On the walls were large paintings of Italy, framed in heavy gold frames. On the mantlepiece, above the marble fireplace, there were cups and trophies, and at the far end was a great wooden desk, on which stood a large gold pen-stand.

"Yes," said Mr Pipelli, as if reading their thoughts. "It is a splendid room, and I have indeed made a great deal of money out of spaghetti."

"I didn't mean to stare," John said apologetically. "It's just that I've never seen . . ."

"But you are here to stare," Mr Pipelli

47

BEST
SPAGHETTI
EVER

protested. "That's why I invited you. Today you may stare and stare as much as you like, and nobody will think it the slightest bit odd!"

48

The driver had been right. Both John and Nicky liked Mr Pipelli immediately. Whenever he spoke he smiled, and when he wasn't speaking, his eyes twinkled with merriment. He was just the sort of person who would run a competition like this, and he was just the sort of person who would make sure that the winners had fun.

"Well," said Mr Pipelli, rubbing his hands together. "Let's go and take a look at the works. I've been in the spaghetti business for twenty years, you know, and I feel as excited by what goes on here as I was the day I started. So let's not wait any longer! Let's go and take a look at how spaghetti is made!"

They walked out of Mr Pipelli's office and made their way along a passageway that led into the heart of the factory. At the end of the passageway there was a door, which Mr Pipelli opened with a flourish.

"In this very room," he said, his voice lowered in awe, "we see the very beginnings of spaghetti."

John and Nicky craned their necks to see beyond Mr Pipelli. They were standing in the entrance to a large room in the centre of which stood a gigantic mound of flour. From this mound, people in white overalls were taking heaped shovels to pour into great metal mixers. As the flour was shovelled in, white clouds rose like steam, making the faces of the workers seem as pale as if they had just seen ghosts.

"A dusty business at this stage," remarked Mr Pipelli, taking out a large silk handkerchief with which to remove the fine layer of flour that had already settled on the front of his suit.

John and Nicky followed the spaghetti manufacturer as he led them across to the mixing machines. At the side of each bowl there was a woman with a watering can. As each spadeful of flour was put into the bowl, she tipped her can over the edge and poured in a stream of thick, greenish liquid.

"Olive oil," explained Mr Pipelli. "It's very important in the making of spaghetti. And these ladies know exactly how much olive oil to put in each bowl. They all come from the same part of Italy – every one of them – where everybody, absolutely everybody, knows all there is to know about olive oil!"

John looked at the woman beside the bowl, who smiled at him, winked, and before he knew what was happening had tossed back her head, opened her mouth, and poured a stream of olive oil right down her throat!

John looked aghast, but Mr Pipelli just laughed.

"Don't worry about that," he said. "They live on olive oil. There's nothing they like better."

He nodded to the woman as they began to move on.

"Thank you, Olivia," he said. "And do take the rest of the day off, if you wish!"

As they went on, Mr Pipelli turned to the children and whispered.

"She won't take the day off," he explained. "She loves her job so much that she'll want to stay. This is a very happy factory, you see!"

~ 6 ~
Things Go Wrong

"Next," said Mr Pipelli as they prepared to leave the room. "Next we shall see what happens to the dough. This is the really exciting part!"

Wondering what they were going to see next, John and Nicky followed their host through a door into another large room. This room was much noisier, as it was filled by a large machine, which was shuddering and shaking and making the most peculiar squelchy sound.

"This," said Mr Pipelli proudly, "is the actual spaghetti-making machine! This is the very heart of the factory."

John and Nicky gazed at the giant machine. At one end, there was an open bowl, almost the size of a swimming pool, into which the dough which had been mixed next door was being loaded in great sticky globules. From that, a number of thick pipes led into the machine itself, one side of which was covered with a

variety of dials and levers. Then, at the far end of the machine, more people in white uniforms were bustling about, taking strands of finished spaghetti in their hands like bundles of wool.

"This is the spaghetti spinner," explained Mr Pipelli, proudly. "It is, in fact, the most advanced and expensive spaghetti spinner in the world. Not only can it make spaghetti, it can make macaroni, canelloni, tagliatelli and every other shape of pasta you could dream of!" Mr Pipelli's expression had become dreamy.

"Just the names of all the pastas make my mouth water," he said. "Just think of them! Capellini! Quadretinni! Nastrini! Farfallette!"

He closed his eyes in ecstasy before he remembered that he had visitors and came back to earth. With a look of pride, he pointed to the other side of the room.

"And that's the finished product being hung up to dry," he said. "That's only a week's output of spaghetti – enough to supply an entire city for at least a year!"

John and Nicky gazed at the towering white racks on which the spaghetti had been hung up to dry. You could get lost in that, John thought; and if you did, it would be like being in a spaghetti forest.

Mr Pipelli made his way towards the machine, beckoning the children to follow him.

"These dials control the shape," he said, pointing to a line of the buttons and wheels along the side of the machine.

He turned and whispered in Nicky's ear.

"Have you ever seen twisty spaghetti?" he asked.

Nicky shook her head.

"Then watch," said Mr Pipelli, fiddling with one of the dials.

As the dials turned, the noise inside the machine seemed to change briefly and within a few seconds the most amazing twisty spaghetti began to emerge at the other end.

Mr Pipelli turned to John, beaming with pride.

"I'm the only person in the world who makes that," he said. "Now, what about you? Would you like to try a special shape?"

John reached forward to the dial and began to turn it gingerly.

"A little bit more to the left," prompted Mr Pipelli. "Now to the right."

Nicky watched with fascination as the machine began to respond to her brother's instructions.

"It's round!" she cried out. "Round spaghetti!"

Mr Pipelli cast a glance at the place where the spaghetti was emerging.

"Well!" he exclaimed. "What an interesting shape. Perhaps we'll have to make more of that."

John craned his neck to see the results of his adjustment. The round spaghetti was certainly very interesting, and tasty-looking too, but perhaps it was a little bit too short.

"Can I make it longer?" he asked.

"Anything you wish," said Mr Pipelli. "Just pull that lever over there."

John gave the lever a tug.

"Not so far!" shouted Mr Pipelli, but it was too late. The machine gave a shudder

and started to whine. Almost
immediately, from the other
end, immensely long strands
of spaghetti began
to shoot out.
In fact, they
were so long that
they appeared to
have no end at all.
"Cable spaghetti!"
moaned Mr Pipelli,
rushing around
and throwing his hands in the air. "Exactly
what every spaghetti manufacturer dreads
more than anything else!"

It took Mr Pipelli a minute or two

to recover himself. During this time, the machine continued to spew out the strands of endless spaghetti. At the other end, the spaghetti workers frantically tried to pick up the growing mounds of spaghetti strands, but no sooner did they manage to shift some of them than the machine produced more than they had taken away. It was a hopeless task.

Then, when at last he began to calm down, Mr Pipelli managed to find the switch which turned the machine off. With a last heave and gurgle, the giant spaghetti-making device squeezed out the last few feet of spaghetti and became silent.

Mr Pipelli mopped his brow.

"Don't worry," he said to John. "That wasn't your fault. This machine's been faulty for a good few months. It was bound to do that sooner or later."

John was relieved to hear this. He had been certain it was all his fault.

"We'll have to try and deal with all that spaghetti," said Mr Pipelli. "Then I intend to do something about fixing this machine."

Mr Pipelli now took John and Nicky to stand beside the vast mountain of spaghetti.

"It's going to be rather difficult," he said despondently. "We'll have to find the ends of the strands – then we'll have to roll this all up. That's the only way to do it."

John and Nicky looked at the spaghetti. It seemed like an impossible task to sort out the muddle of strands, and yet, as John looked, he saw what looked like an end. Cautiously he reached down and picked it up.

"Well done!" said Mr Pipelli. "Now just pull on it."

John did as he was told and gradually drew out a long strand of spaghetti. It seemed to go on forever and soon he was standing at the other end of the room, linked to the pile of spaghetti by a long, slithery strand.

While this was happening, Nicky had spotted another end which she took hold of and began to draw out. Soon she was standing by John's side while Mr Pipelli went off to a storeroom to look for something to wind it round. After a few minutes he came back, carrying an empty barrel. Then, closely supervised by Mr Pipelli, the children began the slippery task of winding the still-wet spaghetti on to the barrel. It was slow work, as the spaghetti kept getting twisted and knotted up, but at last it was finished and the mountain of spaghetti began to look much smaller.

"We shall let the spaghetti workers

do all the rest," said Mr Pipelli, who was beginning to look very much more cheerful. "Now, let's take a look at this machine. Does either of you know anything about machinery?"

John and Nicky shook their heads. They could put the chain back on a bicycle – but you would have to know a great deal more than that to be able to fix something as complicated as a spaghetti-making machine.

Mr Pipelli looked slightly disappointed.

"Oh dear," he said. "I don't know much about it myself. Still, we can have a go!"

~ 7 ~
Tangled Up

John and Nicky watched quietly as Mr Pipelli picked up a screwdriver and began to unscrew a metal plate on the side of the machine.

"This is the inspection hatch," he explained cheerfully. "It allows us to get inside the works."

John looked doubtfully at Nicky and gulped. What would be inside that great, gleaming machine? And what could they possibly do inside it? Was Mr Pipelli quite sure that it was turned off completely?

Mr Pipelli unscrewed the last screw and put the screwdriver down. Then, carefully taking hold of the edges of the plate, he took it off and laid it down on the floor.

John and Nicky peered through the hatch.

"It's very dark inside," ventured John. "Perhaps we should call a mechanic. He might know where everything is."

Mr Pipelli chuckled. "Why go to all that trouble and expense?" he said breezily. "Most machines are quite simple once you work out what's what. And as for the darkness, there's a torch here. So let's go in."

Mr Pipelli led the way, and he was followed by Nicky. John brought up the rear.

"I'm scared," whispered Nicky. "What if somebody turned the machine on while we were in here?"

John did not try to answer her question. Yet there was no doubt in his mind that they would be in very serious trouble if that happened. All about them there were rollers, sifters, crushers and squeezers. The squeezers looked particularly dangerous, and John thought that anybody who got caught up in one of those would stand a very good chance of looking rather like a piece of spaghetti when they eventually got him out.

"You've no need to worry about that," said Mr Pipelli jovially. "It's impossible to turn the machine on when the inspection hatch is open. Now, we've got to locate the bit that controls the length. Can anybody see it?"

John looked up and at that precise moment a large blob of unsqueezed spaghetti dough fell down the back of his neck.

"Perhaps we should be wearing overalls," said Mr Pipelli, noticing what had happened. "Still, one can't expect to visit a spaghetti factory and not get a little bit of spaghetti here and there!"

Mr Pipelli flashed his torch about him. Suddenly he let out a cry of triumph.

"That's it," he said. "That's where the problem is."

The children looked at the place where the beam of light was resting. High up at the top of the machine, the spaghetti had become hopelessly tangled. It was like a giant ball of knitting that had gone terribly wrong.

Mr Pipelli passed the torch to John to

hold while he tried to pull down the tangle, but try as he might he could not quite reach high enough. After he had failed three times he stood back and scratched his head.

"I know what we'll do," he said, after a while. "You climb on my shoulders, John, and we'll do it that way."

Nicky held the torch while John clambered on to Mr Pipelli's shoulders. Then, as Mr Pipelli moved into position, John began to tug at the mess of spaghetti.

It was not easy work. The spaghetti was sticky and had wound itself round and round in a maze of loops and knots. John tugged and pulled, only pausing to wipe strands of spaghetti off his face. And all the time, he heard Mr Pipelli huffing and puffing beneath him, trying to keep him in the right position. Then, just as he had pulled off the last strand, Mr Pipelli's legs gave out from underneath him and John found himself tumbling down, closely followed by the great ball of spaghetti he had just dislodged.

The spaghetti was soft, of course, which was a good thing, but when John got up he was covered in it from head to toe.

"I'm terribly sorry," said Mr Pipelli, nonetheless still sounding very cheerful. "But at least we've fixed the machine. I'm sure it'll work now!"

"But what about me?" John mumbled from somewhere within the tangle of spaghetti. "I'm afraid I'm all tied up."

Mr Pipelli flashed the torch over John.

"I see," he said. "Yes, well maybe we should do something about you. Now, I'll just start pulling on this piece here . . ."

Mr Pipelli took hold of a strand of spaghetti and began to tug. As he did so, John felt the spaghetti slithering around him, like the coils of an impossibly long snake.

"That's it!" said Mr Pipelli enthusiastically. "It's coming away nicely."

Mr Pipelli spoke too soon. Although

the spaghetti had begun to move, it had also begun to tighten.

"Please stop," John called out. "It's tying me up so that I can't move."

Mr Pipelli shook his head.

"We'll have to get you out of here somehow," he said. "Then we can have a better look at the problem."

Helped by Nicky, Mr Pipelli managed to half roll, half push John out of the hatch and back into the factory. The spaghetti workers stood round, gazing at John, scratching their heads.

"Can anybody think of a way to get him out of there?" asked Mr Pipelli. "If we pull at the spaghetti it seems just to get worse."

The spaghetti workers whispered among themselves. They had seen all sorts of things happen in the spaghetti factory. They remembered the day when Mr Pipelli dropped his hat into the spaghetti machine and had watched helplessly as it had come out the other end in long strands of material. They all remembered that very well and still talked about it whenever they saw their employer wearing anything on his head. In fact, one of the spaghetti wor- kers had called her new baby Cappello, which means "hat" in Italian – just to remind her of that marvellous incident. Yes, they had seen many strange things, but never anything quite as strange as this.

As they were standing about, wondering how they could possibly get John out of the tangle, one of the women suddenly stepped forward and whispered something in Mr Pipelli's ear. It was Olivia.

Mr Pipelli listened gravely, stroked his chin, and then nodded.

"That might just work, Olivia," he said. "You just go and fetch the – you know what I mean – and we'll try."

Nicky tugged at Mr Pipelli's sleeve.

"What are you going to do?" she asked timidly. "You're not going to hurt him are you? Aunt Rebecca will be furious if you do."

Mr Pipelli patted her gently on the shoulder.

"Of course not," he said reassuringly. Then, whispering, he went on to explain. "Olivia suggested that we —" his eyes glistened with mischief "— that we pour olive oil all over him. In that way he'll be slippery enough to wriggle his way out of the spaghetti! Now, isn't that a brilliant idea?"

Before Nicky had the chance to reply, Olivia had returned. Fortunately, John could not see out of the spaghetti tangle and so he was unable to watch them raise the large can over his head and begin to pour. The first thing he knew of it was

when he felt the cold, slippery oil slithering its way all over him.

"Now!" shouted Mr Pipelli. "Wriggle!"

John did as he was told and, after a few
moments of wriggling and hopping, he
felt himself begin to slip out of the tangle.
With a final shiver and shake, he popped
out of the tangle and was free. As he did
so, all the spaghetti workers raised a cheer
of delight.

John was thrilled to be free of the
spaghetti. In fact, he was so pleased, that
he hardly noticed the fact that he was
covered, not only with little bits of
spaghetti, but with olive oil too.

Mr Pipelli beamed with pleasure.

"Now, we can try the machine again," he said. "Let's see if we've fixed it."

It took only one press on the button. With a great whirring the machine came back to life, working perfectly.

"We did it!" shouted Mr Pipelli. "Everybody take a day's holiday!"

The spaghetti workers gave another rousing cheer and Mr Pipelli turned to John and Nicky.

"And as for you, my friends," he said. "Let's go straight to the factory kitchen and have lunch. I've asked the chef to cook the very best plate of spaghetti he can manage, so I can assure you it should be most delicious."

Mr Pipelli was right. The lunch was even tastier than the one which John and Nicky had eaten in the restaurant. There was not just one plate of spaghetti for each person – there were six! There was:

For the first course:

Spaghetti with special cheese sauce, made out of Swiss cheese with holes. The spaghetti was threaded through the holes of the cheese and tied in bows!

For the second course:

A single strand of spaghetti ten yards long. This strand was curled round and round on the plate and had to be sucked up into the mouth and swallowed all in one piece!

For the third course:

Spaghetti which was plain on the outside but which had the sauce inside the hollow centre. Many tried to make such spaghetti, but only Mr Pipelli could do it.

For the fourth course:

Indian cobra spaghetti. This spaghetti stood up on end like a cobra. It swayed as you tried to eat it, but was very delicious when caught.

For the fifth course:

Needle spaghetti. This spaghetti was so thin that you could suck it into your mouth through the spaces in between your teeth!

For the sixth, and final course:

Ordinary spaghetti in the most delicious red sauce imaginable. There was oodles of sauce, which had to be slurped up with the spaghetti. Everybody made a great noise doing this, and got covered with sauce, more or less from head to toe. Second helpings were served – twice!

Afterwards, as full and as happy as they had ever been in their lives, the children were led by Mr Pipelli to the front door and ushered into a waiting car.

"Thank you so much for all your help," he said, as he shook hands with them. "And perhaps we shall meet again one day. After all, who knows what life can bring?"

The car drew away from the factory, with Mr Pipelli still standing on the steps, waving his handkerchief at his departing guests. Inside the car, John and Nicky were happier than they had been for years. It didn't matter that John had a blob of spaghetti dough lodged down the back of his shirt. It did not matter that the rest of his clothes were covered with sticky strands of spaghetti as well as being soaked in olive oil. Nor did it matter that Nicky's dress was splattered with hundreds of reminders of the red sauce. It had been a marvellous, exciting day and they both knew they would remember every moment of it forever.

~ 8 ~
Aunt Rebecca Gets
to Work

"Look at you!" hissed Aunt Rebecca, quivering with rage. "Just look at you!"

John hung his head. He had to admit that he looked a bit of a sight, covered as he was with spaghetti, but surely it would all wash off easily enough?

"And as for you, Nicky," Aunt Rebecca went on. "What were you doing letting your brother get himself into such a state? And look at your dress – ruined!"

"I was holding a torch!" Nicky said timidly. "Mr Pipelli had John on his shoulders, you see –"

"On his what?" cried Aunt Rebecca. "You both obviously have a great deal of explaining to do!"

John tried to tell his aunt about what happened, but it only seemed to make matters worse. At the end of his explanation, her face was stormy with anger.

"I should have known that something

like this would happen," she said. "Nothing good could be expected of a spaghetti factory! And as for that Mr Pipelli, I very much hope that he has a good explanation when I see him tomorrow."

"You're seeing him tomorrow?" Nicky asked. "But why?"

"To complain," snapped Aunt Rebecca. "Do you think I'm going to let him get away with all this?"

John and Nicky remained silent. When Aunt Rebecca was in that sort of mood, they knew there was nothing they could do to persuade her otherwise.

The next day Aunt Rebecca told John and Nicky to get ready to accompany her

to Mr Pipelli's factory. They were very unwilling to go, as the last thing they wanted to do was to complain to the generous and likeable Mr Pipelli, but their aunt insisted.

They arrived at the factory in sunken spirits.

"It's going to be awful," Nicky whispered to John. "She's going to make a terrible scene."

"I know," said John under his breath. "And Mr Pipelli will think that we put her up to it."

The man at the factory gate tried to tell Aunt Rebecca that it would be impossible for her to see Mr Pipelli, but she brushed him aside.

"If you don't show me to his office," she said, "then I shall find my own way there."

The man looked Aunt Rebecca up and down and decided that she was not a person to be trifled with. Reluctantly he led the three of them to the door marked, THE BOSS.

Aunt Rebecca knocked once, but did not wait for an answer. Throwing the door wide open, she burst into Mr Pipelli's room and marched up to the astonished spaghetti manufacturer's desk.

Mr Pipelli sprang to his feet and, hiding his surprise, bowed to Aunt Rebecca.

"My dear lady," he said, reaching for her hand. "How kind of you to call on me. I take it that you're the aunt of my two friends."

Aunt Rebecca stopped in her tracks.

"Please," said Mr Pipelli, kissing her hand. "Please allow me to offer you a chair."

By now, Aunt Rebecca, overcome by the politeness and charm of the famous spaghetti manufacturer, was completely incapable of complaining.

"Actually," she began. "I was rather . . . er . . . rather cross . . ."

She stopped. Mr Pipelli had now seated her in a chair and had offered her a peppermint from a silver bowl on his desk.

"I don't eat sweets," said Aunt Rebecca.

"But how wise!" said Mr Pipelli. "If only other people would do the same as you."

Aunt Rebecca looked suspiciously at Mr Pipelli.

"But I don't see how you can say that," she said. "After all, you make all that spaghetti which people cover with red sauce and terrible things like that."

Mr Pipelli waved a hand in the air.

"Well perhaps you could help me," he said, smiling in a charming way. "I've always wanted to make a healthier sort of spaghetti, but I've never found quite the right recipe."

For the first time that day, Aunt Rebecca smiled.

"Perhaps I could help," she said, warming to his idea. "Perhaps I could invent . . . carrot-flavoured spaghetti!"

Mr Pipelli clapped his hands together.

"My dear lady," he said. "What a brilliant idea! Please, please, do that for me. I should be most grateful if you did." And at that, Mr Pipelli rose to his feet and kissed her hand again, making Aunt Rebecca look down at the floor and blush.

Aunt Rebecca was quite silent on the way back home. When they reached the house, the two children watched her as she made straight for the kitchen and closed the door behind her.

"She really means it," said Nicky. "She really intends to invent carrot-flavoured spaghetti."

"It'll taste awful," said John. "The only people who will even think about eating it will be the members of the Carrot and Nut League."

Aunt Rebecca remained in the kitchen for the rest of the day. She came out briefly at lunch time, to hand the two children a plate of lettuce sandwiches to eat, but she seemed too preoccupied to talk.

At four o'clock in the afternoon, John began to worry. He knocked at the door and asked her if she was all right, but he received no more than a grunt in reply. At five o'clock he knocked again, and this time Aunt Rebecca opened the door and peered out at him.

"Yes," she said. "What is it?"

"I was wondering if you were all right," John said. "We haven't seen you all day."

Aunt Rebecca dried her hands on her apron.

"I'm perfectly all right," she said. "And dinner will be at the normal time – seven on the dot." Then she closed the door.

~ 9 ~
Mr Pipelli Comes for Lunch

John and Nicky were sitting at the table at five minutes before seven. At seven o'clock exactly, the door from the kitchen opened and Aunt Rebecca came out carrying a large bowl from which a small cloud of steam was rising. It was obvious

to the children that this was not a dish of raw onions or lettuce salad. But what could it be?

"Spaghetti," announced Aunt Rebecca simply. "You tell me how much you like the stuff, and so I've made you some."

Nicky's mouth fell open with surprise.

"Spaghetti?" she exclaimed. "Real spaghetti?"

"Yes," said Aunt Rebecca proudly. "What is more, this is the first bowl, the very first bowl, of carrot-flavoured spaghetti. I've just invented it, and I shall introduce that Pipelli man to it tomorrow."

John and Nicky watched suspiciously as the newly-invented spaghetti was ladled on to their plates. It looked like ordinary spaghetti in shape, but it was undeniably carrot-coloured.

"Eat up," said Aunt Rebecca. "It won't taste nearly so good if you let it get cold."

Reluctantly John and Nicky wound the

yellow strands around their forks and then passed it to their mouths. Then they looked down at their plates, and after that at one another.

"Well?" asked Aunt Rebecca. "What do you think?"

"It's marvellous," said John.

"Wonderful!" said Nicky.

And they meant it. Aunt Rebecca had invented the most delicious spaghetti they had ever tasted. It was a miracle, and they had been right there in the house when it had happened. Without a break they finished off the rest of the spaghetti before them and then passed the empty plates to their aunt for more.

"My word!" exclaimed Aunt Rebecca, her face breaking out into a contented smile. "That's the first time you've asked for more – ever!"

Aunt Rebecca telephoned Mr Pipelli the next morning and invited him to the house for lunch. He agreed to come, and when he arrived at the front door he had presents for everyone. John and Nicky each received a fountain pen with a real gold nib, and for Aunt Rebecca there was a bouquet of red roses. She became quite speechless when he gave these to her, and when he bent and kissed her hand again the children noticed that she blushed so much that she made the roses look pale.

The new spaghetti was served for lunch. Everyone eagerly awaited Mr Pipelli's reaction, and when it came they were not disappointed. As he took the first mouthful his eyes rolled up to the ceiling in ecstasy. Then, on the second mouthful, he threw his hands up, leapt to his feet, and tossed his table napkin out of the window in his excitement.

"It is magnificent!" he said, when he had recovered enough to speak. "We shall start manufacturing this spaghetti immediately."

He sat down and looked seriously at Aunt Rebecca.

"You have done the world of spaghetti

making a great service," he said solemnly. "And that will never be forgotten. Never!"

"What a nice man you are," said Aunt Rebecca, "for a spaghetti manufacturer," she added. "Would you care to join us for lunch tomorrow?"

Mr Pipelli nodded his head enthusiastically and said that this would give him the greatest pleasure. John felt that he should warn him that lunch could well be raw onions and seaweed, but he did not have the opportunity to speak to him privately.

John need not have worried. Mr Pipelli sat at the table the following day and ate his raw onions with every appearance of pleasure. At the end, to the astonishment of the two children, he asked for more.

"Quite delicious," Mr Pipelli said, smacking his lips rather loudly. "And so positively good for the system."

"Absolutely," said Aunt Rebecca, as she ladled more onions on to her visitor's plate.

Mr Pipelli came back to lunch the next day, and the day after that. He and Aunt Rebecca seemed to get on very well, and they always took a walk round the garden after the meal. There Mr Pipelli would pick roses from Aunt Rebecca's rose-bushes (something she normally never allowed anybody to do) and would present them to her with a low bow.

Finally, exactly one week later, Mr Pipelli announced that he had invited Aunt Rebecca to marry him and that she had agreed. They would be married the following Saturday and would all move into his mansion near the spaghetti factory.

"Your charming aunt will become Mrs Pipelli," he said proudly. "And you, my dear children, will become my step-nephew and step-niece. You can stay with us until your parents have found all the volcanoes they can. After all, there can't be that many. That is, of course, if you agree to this little change in your lives."

"Of course we do," shouted Nicky, and kissed Aunt Rebecca on the cheek. Aunt Rebecca smiled. She seemed much less severe now — it was almost as if she had caught Mr Pipelli's habit of beaming with pleasure at everything he saw.

Because she was in such a good mood, later that day John decided to ask Aunt Rebecca about the last time she had been engaged to be married.

"It was all a very long time ago," she explained. "He was a pastry chef, you know — a very good one. He was a kind man too."

"Then what happened?" asked John. "Did he run away?"

For a moment or two Aunt Rebecca looked sorrowful again, as if she were remembering something rather sad.

"No," she said. "He didn't run away. It's just that he was rather . . . greedy. In fact, he was terribly, terribly greedy. When we ate meals together, he would take things from my plate and pop them into his mouth. I don't think he even knew he was doing it."

She paused, dabbing at a tear which had appeared in the corner of her eye.

"He made our wedding cake himself," she said. "It was the most beautiful cake you can imagine. It was covered with at least four bowls of marzipan and there were six tiers of white icing. Then, the day before the wedding, when I knew that the cake would be finished, I went round to look at it. And that's when I changed my mind."

John wondered what Aunt Rebecca could possibly have seen to make her call off the wedding.

"There he was," she said. "He was sitting in his kitchen, looking very pleased with himself. And do you know what he had done? He had eaten the cake – every last crumb of it!"

"All six tiers?" asked Nicky, astonished

that one person could be so greedy as to eat his own wedding cake — before the wedding.

"Yes," said Aunt Rebecca grimly. "And when he saw me, he looked very guilty. So I said to him: Octavius Hunt (for that was what he was called), you will have to find somebody else to marry you I'm afraid! You are far, far too greedy for me!"

"Mr Pipelli would never do anything like that," said John.

At the mention of Mr Pipelli's name, Aunt Rebecca cheered up.

"Of course he wouldn't," she said, closing her eyes dreamily. "What a marvellous man he is!"

From that day on, Aunt Rebecca was a different person. She never scowled, she was cheerful all day, and everything about her seemed so much brighter. But, most remarkable of all, was the change which occurred in Aunt Rebecca's views on food. Of course John and Nicky didn't expect her to give up all her ideas – and she still believed in the beneficial effect of carrots and onions – but she did seem to be a little more prepared to accept that there was nothing really wrong with spaghetti, even if you put some rather thick sauce on it. And that, as far as John and Nicky were concerned, was a major breakthrough.

On the day before the wedding, Aunt Rebecca went so far as to cook them some of the ordinary spaghetti which Mr Pipelli had given her. She tasted it herself, and had to admit that it was delicious, even if not quite as delicious as her own carrot-flavoured variety.

"I suppose I should eat this from now on," she said, a little bit hesitantly. "After all, as from tomorrow I shall be the new Mrs Pipelli, and I shall have responsibilities towards the spaghetti industry."

John tried not to catch Nicky's eye. If he did, he knew that it would be difficult not to smile.

The wedding was a splendid affair.

Aunt Rebecca carried a bouquet of yellow flowers which Nicky had specially picked for her from the garden of Mr Pipelli's mansion, and Mr Pipelli beamed more than you would have thought it possible for anybody to beam. Outside, there were crowds of spaghetti workers who cheered lustily as the happy couple emerged.

"Well done!" they shouted in unison. "And may you be happy for the rest of your lives."

"Thank you, all," responded Mr Pipelli. "And take one week's extra holiday, starting today."

This led to an even greater commotion,

which brought the traffic to a standstill and made people for miles around open their windows to see what great event was happening.

John and Nicky watched all this, their hearts full of happiness. Then, as a large car drew up to take Mr Pipelli and Aunt Rebecca off on their honeymoon to Italy, John and Nicky joined the happy spaghetti workers to throw confetti on the newly-weds.

But it was not confetti they threw – it was spaghetti – which is an unusual thing to throw at a wedding. But on this occasion it was just right.

TEACHER TROUBLE

~ 1 ~
First Day at School

Jenny was very tall. She had always been tall, right from the very beginning, and now that she was ten she was almost as tall as most grown-ups, and a good deal taller than some. This was often very useful. She always came first at high

jump, and in libraries she was able to reach books from the shelves that nobody else could reach. The best books were always to be found there, she thought.

But there were times when it was

certainly a bit of a nuisance being tall. It was sometimes quite difficult to get clothes that were just the right size, and the desks at school often didn't have quite enough knee room. And then there were occasions when being tall led to quite remarkable things, as happened with the great mistake.

It all started when Jenny had to change schools. Her family had moved to a new town and Jenny and her brother had to go to new schools. Her brother was older than she was, and so he was to go to one school while she was to go to another. Jenny, in fact, had a choice of two schools.

The schools wrote to her mother and

sent their brochures. Each had a picture on the front page and inside you could read about what the schools were like. There was nothing particularly unusual about these schools, but there was a very curious thing about their names. One was called the Pond Street School and the other was called Street Pond School. This was very strange, as they were not far from one another and Jenny thought that it must have led to lots of mix-ups.

And she was right. There had been lots of confusion. For example, the mail for the principal of Street Pond School often went to the principal of Pond Street School, and the other way round. Sometimes Pond

Street School got a bill which was meant for Street Pond School – and paid it – which meant that when the mistake was discovered, Street Pond School had to pay Pond Street School back.

Sometimes Street Pond School won a competition, but the papers announced that Pond Street School had won. This made Street Pond School furious, and there would have to be an announcement in the papers that Pond Street School hadn't won anything at all, which made Pond Street School furious – because they sometimes won things anyway. So it was all very confusing.

Jenny could not make up her mind

which school she preferred, and so her mother chose for her and Jenny agreed with the choice.

"Pond Street School looks fine," said her mother. "I think you should go to that one."

Jenny agreed. The name sounded quite nice and she was sure that she would make new friends there.

On her first morning at the new school, Jenny got everything ready in good time. She packed her bag with the new pencil case she had bought and with all the other things that she was bound to need. Her mother had insisted that she dress as smartly as she could on her first day at school, and had made her wear a dress which Jenny didn't really like.

"It's such an old-fashioned dress," Jenny complained. "It makes me look so old."

"Nonsense," her mother retorted. "You can't go to your new school wearing jeans and a scruffy T-shirt. You look very good in that dress."

Jenny knew that it was no good arguing with her mother when she had made up her mind about something. So she put on the old-fashioned dress and went down to breakfast. Then, when she was finally ready to leave the house, her father and mother both wished her good luck.

"I'll drive you to school," her father offered.

"No thank you," said Jenny. "I know the way . . . I think."

Jenny waved to her parents and began the short walk that would lead her to the front gate of her new school. She felt very excited, and a bit anxious, as you always do when you are about to start a new school and aren't quite sure what everybody will be like. She wondered whether she would meet many new friends there. She had had very good friends at her last school and she had been sorry to leave them. She hoped that the pupils at her new school would be as nice, or at least almost as nice.

As she drew near to the new school she began to walk more slowly. It was far bigger than her last school, she thought, and there were many more pupils milling about. And where was she meant to go? Should she walk straight in the main entrance and try to find the office, or should she look for some children who were about her age and just follow them in? She could always ask somebody to help her, of course, but she didn't know anybody and everyone except her seemed to be busy talking to their friends.

Jenny arrived at the entrance to the school and looked about her. Nobody was taking any notice of her and so she decided just to stand there for a little while and see what happened. Perhaps one of the teachers would come and ask her her name and then take her to her classroom.

"Good morning."

Jenny spun round. One of the teachers had come up and was standing right behind her. Jenny noticed that she was taller than the teacher, who was smiling at her in a friendly manner.

"So there you are," said the teacher. "We've been expecting you."

"Oh, good," said Jenny. She was pleased to hear that they knew she was coming. This meant that she wouldn't have to ask her way after all.

"If you'd like to come along with me," said the teacher, "I'll show you where your classroom is."

Jenny followed as the teacher led the way. They went into the building and walked along a long corridor past the open doors of several classrooms. Jenny noticed that most of the classrooms had now filled up with pupils and that lessons were just about to begin.

"By the way," said the teacher. "I didn't introduce myself. My name is Alison."

Jenny was rather surprised. Alison sounded like a first name, and it was rather odd for a teacher to give her first name to a pupil. Perhaps this was a very friendly school, where everybody called the teachers Mary, or John, or whatever their first names might be. Jenny had heard about schools like that before, but she had never actually been in one.

They stopped outside the door of the last classroom in the corridor.

"Here we are," said the teacher. "This is your classroom."

Jenny looked through the door. The classroom was full, and all the pupils were seated at their desks, looking at her. She wished that she had arrived earlier. Nobody would have paid so much attention to her if she had arrived at the same time as everyone else.

They went into the classroom and everybody stopped talking.

"Good morning class," said the teacher.

As the class replied, Jenny glanced nervously about the room. She was surprised to see that everybody looked younger than she did – at least one or two years younger. *But perhaps I am imagining it*, she thought. *Perhaps it's just because I'm not used to them.*

She looked around the room again. Every single desk was occupied and there did not appear to be a single seat left. She looked at the teacher.

"Excuse me," she said. "Where do I sit?"

The teacher looked at her in surprise, and then smiled.

"Yes," she said. "I'm sorry. The school is a bit crowded. But don't worry, we've kept your seat free."

And with that she pointed to the chair behind the table facing the class. The teacher's seat!

~ 2 ~
Taking the Register

For a moment, Jenny did not know what to think. The teacher had definitely pointed to that chair, and her ears had not been deceiving her when she heard her tell her that she was to sit there. But where was the teacher going to sit herself? Would she walk about the classroom or just stand in the same place all day? Surely she would need to sit down some time.

"Well," said the teacher. "I'll leave you to get on with it. I've got to go and teach my class. But I'll come back when the break bell goes and show you where the staff room is."

Staff room? Why should I need to know where the staff room is? Jenny asked herself. *Perhaps I might have to run an errand for a teacher some time.* But there was still the problem of the chair. Perhaps she should do as she was told and sit in it after all.

Jenny went towards the teacher's chair

and sat in it, feeling very embarrassed as she did so. Yet although everybody was staring at her, nobody was laughing.

"By the way," said the teacher as she left the room. "You'll find the register in the top drawer of the desk. The principal likes it to be called first thing every morning."

Jenny was astonished. Usually teachers called the register, but perhaps this school was different. Well, if that's what they wanted her to do, she could do it for them . . .

The teacher now left the classroom and Jenny opened the top drawer of the desk. There was a large brown book, which she

took out and opened at the first page. There was a list of names, written out in alphabetical order, and against them neat lines of ticks and crosses had been put in.

Everybody was quiet as Jenny called out the first name.

"George Apple," she called.

"Yes," said a boy from the front row. "Yes, I'm here."

Jenny put a tick after George Apple's name.

"Caroline Box," she called.

There was no reply, so Jenny called out the name again in case Caroline Box had not heard.

Still there was no reply. Then a girl sitting at the front put up her hand.

"Please, miss," she said. "Caroline Box isn't well. She lives next door to me and her mother said she had a bad cold."

"Oh, I see," said Jenny, putting a cross against the name. Then she stopped, her hand frozen where it was. The girl had called her "miss"! Why on earth should she do that? It was not as if she was a teacher.

Suddenly, and with a terrible bump, it all fell into place. No! Surely the teacher couldn't have mistaken her . . . for a teacher! It was quite impossible. And yet, everything seemed to point to this. She had been shown the teacher's chair. She had been told about the staff room. She had been asked to call the register.

Jenny's mind raced as she thought about the terrible mistake that had been made. She was tall, of course, and people often said she could be mistaken for a grown-up. But nobody had ever actually made that mistake, and certainly nobody had ever mistaken her for a teacher!

They must have been expecting a new teacher, she thought. *Then, when they saw me standing at the gate, they must have thought that I was the person they were waiting for.*

It was an awful mistake to have been made, but it had been made and here she was in charge of a whole class, calling the register! The very thought made Jenny's skin come out in goosebumps. It was the most embarrassing, terrible thing that had ever happened to her. It was a complete and utter nightmare.

Without really thinking of what she was doing, Jenny continued to call the register. Then, when all the names had been called, she replaced the book in the drawer of the desk and took a deep breath.

The simplest thing to do would be to get to her feet and to rush out of the room. She would run out of the school and all the way home and tell her parents all about the terrible mistake.

She looked at the people in front of her. They were all sitting quite still, waiting for her to begin. Somehow it seemed impossible to rise to her feet and run out of the room. Her legs just would not carry her that far, she thought.

"Well," she said suddenly, her voice sounding very small and far away. "What lesson do you normally have at the beginning of the day?"

"Maths," said a boy in the front. "We do mathematics on Monday, Wednesday and Friday. On Tuesday and Thursday we do history."

Jenny thought quickly. At least she was quite good at mathematics – it was her strongest subject in fact. But would she be able to teach it? It was hard enough to be able to do complicated sums, but it must be even more difficult to teach other people how to do them.

"Get out your maths books, then," she said. "Start where you left off and do the whole page."

Desks were opened and maths books were fished out. Then, with a busy murmur, the class got down to work. Jenny sat in her chair and looked about her. *Perhaps I could dash out while they were all working*, she thought. *I could tell them that I was going to get something from the staff room, and run away once I was out of the door.* Yes. That was the way to do it.

She rose to her feet.

"Carry on with your maths," she said, trying to sound as firm as possible. "I've just got to get something from the staff room."

"Please, miss," called out George Apple. "I'll go and fetch it for you."

"No," said Jenny. "You stay here and work. I'll just be a moment."

Not looking behind her, she walked across to the classroom door, opened it, and went out into the corridor. Nobody was about and so she started to walk purposefully towards the door at the far end.

She had got about halfway when she heard footsteps. Somebody was coming round the corner and, in an awful moment of panic, Jenny realised that there was nowhere to hide. She would shortly come face to face with the person who was coming around the corner – whoever that might be.

~ 3 ~
Sent Back to Class

It turned out to be a rather severe-looking woman, a little bit taller than Jenny, wearing small round glasses and with very short, red hair. When she saw Jenny, she fixed her with a firm gaze and walked quickly towards her.

"So," she said. "You're the new teacher. I'm very glad to see you."

Jenny swallowed hard, wondering what to say.

"I'm Miss Ice, the principal," said the woman. "And may I ask where you're going? We normally don't leave our classrooms unattended at this school."

Jenny looked down at the ground. She was completely terrified of this severe-looking woman and, even if she had known what to say, she doubted whether her tongue would work.

"Well?" said the principal. "Are you going back to the classroom?"

Jenny nodded miserably and, under the

principal's suspicious stare, she walked
quickly back to her classroom. Everybody
was still working on their maths when
Jenny got back. The classroom was quiet –
rather unusually so, and Jenny wondered
whether something was going on. Nobody

was whispering to one another and every head was bent over a book. Jenny sat down at her table and looked down at the class. What was the reason for the quiet? Was the maths all that difficult? Surely not.

Suddenly she heard a noise. It was not a loud noise – more of a scuffling sound. She strained her ears to hear it better. It had gone, but then it came back – an odd, scraping sound, rather as if something was scraping at a bit of paper.

Jenny looked behind her. There was nothing there. She turned to face the class again, and she saw that several people were looking up at her. One of them was George Apple, and he was grinning broadly.

"Is there something wrong, miss?" he said.

Jenny shook her head.

"No," she said. "I thought I heard a noise, but I think it's gone."

Everybody looked up now, and Jenny noticed that most of the class was grinning. This was a trick of some kind – she was sure of it.

"I heard a noise too, miss," said George Apple. "I thought it was coming from the drawer in your desk."

Jenny looked down. The noise was there again, and yes, it did seem to be coming from the drawer.

"Why not open the drawer and take

a look," suggested George Apple. "Just to check."

Jenny reached out and opened the drawer, and the moment she did so out jumped the largest brown rat she had ever seen. Jenny pushed her chair back as quickly as she could, letting out a scream that made the windows rattle.

"A rat!" she shrieked. "A great big rat."

The rat had now landed on her table and was scurrying around, wondering what all the fuss was.

"You've got a rat on your table, miss," said George Apple helpfully. "Should I take it away for you?"

Jenny nodded miserably. She had always been scared of rats and when it had popped its head out of the drawer her heart had almost stopped. She sat quite still as George Apple sauntered up to her desk, picked up the rat by its tail, and took it back to his desk. Then he slipped it into his bag, and sat back at his desk.

Every eye was on Jenny. Some people were trying not to laugh, and succeeding. Others were giggling under their breath. Everybody thought it very funny – except Jenny. She had no idea what to do. Should she report George Apple to the principal? If she did that though, she would have to face Miss Ice again and that was the last thing she wanted to do. So she decided to get back to maths and to forget about rats for the time being.

"Will you give us the answers now?" asked one of the girls. "I hope I've got everything right!"

Jenny took the girl's book and looked at it. The work seemed rather difficult to her, and she was not sure if she would be able to do it.

"Well, let's see," she said. "I'll call out the answers and you can all mark your own work."

Reading out from the girl's book, she called out the answers.

"Problem number one – the answer is two thousand three hundred and forty-two."

Nobody said it wasn't, so Jenny moved on to the next problem, and the problem after that. Each time she called out the answer she saw in the girl's exercise book, and each time, it seemed to her, she had the good luck to be quite correct.

"Thank you," she said to the girl as she handed her book back. "You're obviously very good at maths. Well done."

Now what? They had finished their mathematics, and Jenny did not fancy the idea of doing any more. She might not be so lucky this time, and it would be terrible not to be able to do the sums she was meant to be teaching.

An idea came to her.

"Let's do some geography," she said. "Can anybody tell me what the capital of France is?"

"That's easy," several voices called out. "Paris."

"Good," said Jenny. "Now what about Italy? Who knows the capital of Italy?"

Several hands went up, and Jenny pointed to a boy at the back.

"Cairo?" he said.

Everyone roared with laughter.

"That's in Egypt," said George Apple, in disgust. "Everyone knows it's Rome."

Jenny thought quickly. Perhaps she should try something harder.

"What's the capital of . . ." she paused for a moment, trying to think of a country. "Yes, that's a good idea. What's the capital of Australia?"

The word Australia just slipped out, because Australia had somehow come to her mind. But no sooner had she said it than she realised, with a shock, that she had no idea at all what the capital of Australia was. There was a hope, of course, that somebody would know. If only somebody came out with the right answer, then she would not be shown up.

There was a silence. People looked at one another, and one or two scratched their heads. Then a girl in the middle row raised her hand slowly.

Jenny felt a surge of relief.

"Yes," she said. "You look as if you know the answer."

"Sydney," the girl said. Then she added "I think."

Jenny had been very happy to hear "Sydney", but was less pleased to hear the "I think" added on at the end.

Was Sydney the capital city of Australia? Surely it must be, now she came to think of it. It was so big and it had that great big bridge and that wonderful white opera house. When you thought of an Australian town you always thought of Sydney. It must be the capital.

"That's right," she said. "Well done. That was not an easy question."

She was about to ask another question, when she saw George Apple's hand go up.

"Yes, George," she said. "Do you have a question?"

"It's not Sydney," he said simply.

Jenny looked at him. Was he trying to

be troublesome, or could he possibly be right?

"Of course it's Sydney," she said. "We all know it's Sydney, don't we everybody?"

"Yes," said a lot of voices. "Of course it's Sydney."

"It isn't," said George. "I've been there, and I know."

Suddenly everybody became quiet. Jenny stared at George Apple for a few moments. Had he really been there, she wondered, or was he just pretending?

"Well," she said after a while. "If you're so clever and you've been there, you tell us what the right answer is."

"Canberra," said George simply. "Canberra's the capital of Australia. And look, I've got an atlas here to prove it."

Nobody said a word. The whole class stared at Jenny, who said nothing, but just stood there, becoming redder and redder.

Just at that moment, the door behind her opened and another teacher walked in.

"Is your class ready for gym?" she asked. "You're late already."

Jenny heaved a sigh of relief. Sydney, and Canberra, and even Australia itself could be forgotten now. Thank heavens for gym!

~ 4 ~
Trouble in the Gym

The gymnasium was a large hall with a creaky wooden floor and all sorts of exciting equipment arranged around the walls. There were wooden horses for jumping over; ropes to swing on; and wooden bars for climbing up. Jenny was delighted. This was very much better than mathematics or geography. She could really teach gym, she thought, even if she wasn't a real teacher.

The pupils all changed into their gym outfits and stood waiting expectantly for Jenny's instructions.

"Can we play with the sand bags?" one of them asked.

"No," said another. "Can we get the trampoline out?"

Jenny clapped her hands, just as she remembered her last gym teacher doing. Everybody fell silent.

"We'll do some vaulting first," she said, in a firm, gym-teacher-type voice. "Make a long line and jump over the horse one by one."

The members of the class quickly fell into line and started to jump, one by one, over the wooden horse. Most of them did it quite well, although there were one or two who got stuck halfway and had to be helped across.

After everybody had jumped over the horse twice, Jenny decided it was time for something a little bit more adventurous.

"We're going to climb the bars now," she said. "Everybody will climb right up to the top and then climb down again."

They started, one by one, to climb the bars. The first girl went up very quickly, and then shot down again in no time at all. The second was almost as fast, but not quite, but the third was best of all. She climbed up and down so quickly that you could hardly see her. Then it was George Apple's turn.

He was much slower, and clearly felt rather nervous about the whole thing. He took a lot of time to reach the top and then, when he did, he stopped.

"Come down now," Jenny called out. "The next person wants a turn."

George looked down at the floor of the gym and turned quite pale.

"I can't," he said, his voice shaky with fear. "I'm stuck."

"Come on," urged Jenny.
"Just climb down the same way as you climbed up. It's simple."

George gulped and slowly lowered a foot to the rung below. There was a creaking noise and then the sound of snapping. Jenny caught her breath as a large section of the bars gave way beneath George. If he had not been properly stuck before, he certainly was now.

George let out a wail.

"I can't," he shouted out. "The bars have gone!"

Jenny dashed forward and looked up at George. He was right – he was absolutely stuck.

"He's going to die, miss," said George's best friend. "That's the end of him. So sad. Goodbye, George! Can I have your rat?"

"Oh, miss!" wailed one of the girls. "Poor George! He's not all that bad. It'll be an awful pity to lose him!"

Jenny looked about her. She was the teacher, and she would have to save George. But how?

Her gaze fell on the ropes tied up against the opposite wall. Yes, that was the way to do it! She could use the ropes. It was exactly what Tarzan would do, if he were there.

Wasting no time, Jenny ran to the other side of the gym and untied the thickest rope. Then she tucked her skirt up, climbed a short distance up the rope, and pushed herself away from the wall with all her might.

Like the pendulum of a great clock, the rope, with Jenny clinging to it, swung all the way across the gym. There was a gasp from the pupils as Jenny sailed her way across the void, and a sigh as her outstretched hand narrowly missed the terrified George. But Jenny was not put off by failure, and when she swung back to the other side she pushed herself off again.

This time she reached George with no difficulty, and, taking him quite by surprise, wrenched him off the bars with one hand. Then, holding on to him with all her strength, she sailed back on the rope to the other side and then slid down to the ground, George and all.

As her feet touched the floorboards, a great cheer arose from the class.

"Well done!" they shouted. "Well done! You've saved George's life!"

George stood up on his rather shaky legs and dusted himself down.

"Thank you," he said to Jenny. "I'll never forget that. You're a real heroine, miss!"

"Oh, it was nothing," said Jenny, casually. "That's what teachers are for, aren't they?"

George looked down at the floor. He was clearly feeling ashamed of himself.

"Sorry about the rat, miss," he said. "I was just having a bit of fun."

Jenny smiled. "Don't worry about that," she said. "It *was* quite a good joke, I suppose."

*

Everybody was too excited after that to do much more gym, and so they all changed back into their ordinary clothes and began to go back to the classroom. Jenny told them to go in twos, with each person having a partner, and for some reason this seemed to please everybody.

On the way, they saw the principal, or rather, she saw them. She was standing in the doorway to the library, and she frowned crossly as Jenny walked by.

What a horrible person, thought Jenny. *She's obviously very cross about something. I wonder what it can be?*

~ 5 ~
Miss Ice is Taught a Lesson

Jenny was soon to find out why Miss Ice had looked so cross. Just as the class reached their desks again, with everybody talking in an excited way about how George had been rescued by the new teacher, the bell went for break.

As she had promised, Alison, the teacher who had been so friendly earlier on, came back to show Jenny to the staff room. Jenny had to give up any thought of running away now – it would have been very rude to Alison to do that.

She was very worried about going into the staff room, because she thought that she was bound to be found out there. But Alison was very helpful and poured out a cup of tea for her, also giving her first choice of biscuits. Then Jenny sat down, with Alison at her side, and began to drink her tea.

The other teachers were all looking at her, and Jenny felt very awkward about it. But they all seemed quite friendly too, and Jenny soon relaxed.

But not for long.

"Where were you teaching before you came here?" asked one of the other teachers politely.

Jenny had been about to take a sip of her tea, but her hand froze halfway to her lips.

"Er . . ." she began. "Where was I a teacher?"

"That's what I asked," said the other teacher.

Everybody looked expectantly at Jenny, but her mind was a complete blank. Then a place came into her mind, and she blurted it out, relieved that at least she could give some answer.

"Canberra," she said.

"Oh!" exclaimed one of the other teachers. "How interesting. Please tell us all about it."

Jenny felt her cheeks burning red.

"It's in Australia," she said.

Everybody laughed.

"Oh, we know that," said somebody. "But what's it like?"

Jenny looked at the floor. This was terrible. Why had she not run away on the way to the staff room? At least then she would have been spared this terrible nightmare.

"It's very nice there," she said. "What with the sea and everything."

There was a silence. Then one of the teachers sitting at the far end of the room said something.

"Sea?" he snorted. "Canberra's hundreds of miles from the sea."

Jenny looked at him.

"I didn't say it wasn't," she said defiantly.

"But you did," he said. "You said the sea was what made Canberra a nice place."

Jenny shook her head.

"That's not what I meant," she said, trying to sound slightly cross. "I meant that if you don't like the sea, and you want to be far away from it, then Canberra's a good place to be."

A few of the teachers looked a bit puzzled by this, but, to Jenny's great relief, it was at this moment that the principal came in and everybody turned in her direction. She did not look very happy, and Jenny noticed that for some reason the principal was glaring straight at her.

Jenny's heart sank.

"She must know," she said to herself. "She must have found out!"

The principal helped herself to a cup of tea. Then she examined the plate of biscuits, took the largest, most choco-latey one left, and bit into it with a resounding crunch. As she did so, she shot a furious glance at Jenny.

"I saw your class going back after gym," the principal said frostily. "I noticed that they were walking in pairs."

Jenny looked about her for support, but everybody was looking at the principal.

"Yes," she said after a while. "I think they were."

The principal swallowed the last of her biscuit and cleared her throat.

"In this school," she said, her voice still cool, "the pupils always walk single file. That's the way we do it."

"But that's silly!" Jenny blurted out. "That means that they must take twice as long to go anywhere."

As Jenny spoke, some of the other teachers drew in their breath loudly. They seemed to be shocked that anybody was daring to tell the principal that she was wrong and they were watching closely to see what would happen next.

The principal put down her teacup with shaking hands.

"I beg your pardon?" she said. "Did I hear you correctly? Did you say it's actually better to let the pupils walk in pairs? Is that what you're saying?"

Jenny shrugged her shoulders.

"Yes," she said simply. "That's right. After all, it does seem more sensible, doesn't it?"

The principal let out a sound which was half a snort and half a puff of rage.

"That's not the point," she hissed

between clenched teeth. "If I say something is to be done a certain way, then
that's the way it is to be done!"

"But what if it's better to do it another
way?" said Jenny, feeling and sounding
very miserable. "Surely you should do
something the best way rather than do it
another way just because that's the way
it's always been done."

The principal stared at Jenny, her
mouth open in astonishment that anybody
would actually dare to talk like this.

Then, from the other side of the room,
one of the teachers spoke out.

"She's right," he said. "I don't see why
we should always do things the way

they've been done in the past. And anyway, why don't we vote on it?"

"Good idea," said another teacher.

"Yes," said another. "Let's vote."

So the teachers all voted, and everybody, except for the principal, voted to allow the pupils to walk from classroom to classroom in twos, or even threes. The principal was dumbstruck and, after she had finished her tea, she slunk out of the room, looking quite confused and unhappy.

"Thank you," whispered one of the teachers sitting next to Jenny. "You've done what we've all been itching to do for years. You've put Miss Ice in her place! Well done!"

"Let's all celebrate by having another chocolate biscuit," said Alison, reaching for the biscuit plate.

"But Miss Ice said we can only have one a day," said somebody else.

"I don't care," said Alison. "In fact, I'm going to have three!"

All the other teachers agreed, and as they sat around finishing off every chocolate biscuit on the plate, they smiled warmly at Jenny.

"You haven't been here a full day," said somebody, "and already you've changed things for the better."

Jenny didn't know how to reply. She had not meant to offend the principal like that and she hoped that everybody, including Miss Ice, would forget about it as soon as possible. All that she wanted now was to get home and to ask her parents to come to the school to sort out the mistake. But there were still several lessons left to be taught, and she would have to survive those before she could get away. Would it be easy? She had a dreadful feeling it would not.

~ 6 ~
An Unexpected Reaction

The bell went and everyone returned to their classrooms. Jenny found all the pupils in her class already in their seats, looking at her expectantly. They had been most impressed by her rescue of George Apple, and they wondered what this exciting new teacher would have in store for them next.

It was chemistry. Jenny had not planned to have a chemistry lesson — she had not planned to have any lesson, in fact — but when she saw the box marked *Chemistry* she thought it would be a good idea.

Everybody agreed. They watched carefully as she placed the box on her desk and took out the various bowls and bottles inside. There were also jars of chemical powders — red powders, white powders, blue powders — and these she put neatly to one side.

"I shall now teach you some chemistry," she said to the class.

Picking up a jar of white powder, she opened it and peered at it carefully. The powder looked a little bit like sugar, but it smelled quite different. In fact, it smelled like rotten eggs.

"I'm going to mix a bit of this powder with the red powder," Jenny explained. "Then we'll add a bit of the blue powder, just to be on the safe side."

"Why?" called out a boy from the back. "Why are you mixing the powders together?"

Jenny looked at him scornfully.

"Because that's what chemistry is all about," she replied. "And anyway, have you got any better ideas?"

The boy shook his head.

"Well, then," Jenny went on. "Here goes!"

She poured some of the white powder into a dish and then, standing well back, poured a small quantity of red powder in and mixed them up. Nothing happened.

"You've got to put in much more, miss," said one of the girls at the front. "Our last teacher used to put in loads and loads of powder."

"I know," said Jenny crossly. "I'm just testing it to see if it works. I'm going to add much more now."

She took up the jar and tipped the rest of the red powder into the mixture.

Then she stirred it a little with a long glass rod.

Something was happening now. The mixture was beginning to sizzle a bit. Jenny stood a bit further back. You never knew with chemistry – odd things could happen.

And they did. Suddenly there was a puff of smoke and a bang. Jenny gave a start, and a few people let out whistles of surprise. A cloud of green smoke was now rising up from the dish and beginning to fill that corner of the room.

"There," said Jenny triumphantly. "You see, that's chemistry. It works."

The cloud of smoke seemed to be getting bigger and bigger, and every now and then it made a rather strange, popping sound. It was really rather alarming, thought Jenny, but at least it could not go on for ever. Sooner or later the chemicals would calm down and the cloud of thick green smoke would disappear.

It was while Jenny was thinking this that the door of the classroom opened. Jenny turned round to see Miss Ice standing in the doorway, a look of outrage on her face.

"What is happening here?" the principal demanded. "What is the meaning of this . . . this green cloud?"

"Chemistry," called out one of the boys.

"Silence!" hissed the principal. "Miss
. . . Miss whatever your name is, what do
you think you're doing filling the
classroom with green smoke?"

She did not wait for an answer. Striding
forward, she went straight into the middle

of the cloud of green smoke, waving at it with her arms.

"I shall put a stop to this," she spluttered. "I have never seen anything as disgraceful in my . . ."

Her voice broke off. The principal had disappeared into the swirling cloud of smoke and now there was not a single sign of her.

"She's dissolved!" shouted George Apple. "Miss, you've dissolved the principal!"

Oh dear, thought Jenny. *I really shouldn't have tried chemistry. If only I'd stuck to geography.*

Suddenly there was a coughing sound

and the principal reappeared from the cloud, holding the dish of chemicals, which she had now covered with a cloth.

"This is a disgrace!" she stormed. "You could have blown us all up!"

Jenny was about to say how sorry she was, but stopped. There was something funny about the principal, and all the class noticed it too. Her hair, which had been red when she came into the room, was now quite green!

"Excuse me," Jenny said. "I'm very sorry, but your hair . . ."

"Don't you talk about my hair," said the principal. "There's nothing wrong with my hair. You just open all these windows and get the smoke out of the classroom."

Jenny did as she was asked, but as she did so everybody else started laughing. They had tried to conceal their mirth over the principal's funny hair, but it was just too difficult. Soon everyone was holding their sides, tears of laughter streaming down their faces.

Miss Ice stormed out of the classroom, holding the dish of chemicals in her hand. But just before she left, she stopped and turned in Jenny's direction.

"You're dismissed!" she said. "You will leave the school immediately!"

The laughter stopped. Now everybody sat as quiet as mice, looking at Jenny.

"That's not fair!" said George Apple. "You saved my life!"

"You're the best teacher we've ever had," said another. "Please don't go."

Jenny felt touched by these kind remarks, but at the same time she felt very pleased that she had been sacked. Her being a teacher could not last, and she was relieved that it was all over.

But before she went, she thought she would do one last thing.

"Let's have a picnic," she said. "It's far too nice a day to sit inside and do lessons."

~ 7 ~
A Double Mix-up

Out into the school garden they all trooped, taking with them the sandwiches they were meant to have for lunch. They found a good place, and they all sat, enjoying the sunshine and munching sandwiches and crisps. Everybody was very happy.

Jenny sat next to a girl called Lucy, who told her how much she had enjoyed the school day.

"Our last teacher was very nice," said Lucy. "But not nearly as much fun as you are."

Jenny smiled and thanked Lucy. Then Lucy took two lollipops out of her pocket and offered one to Jenny. Jenny was very pleased. Lollipops were her favourite sweet, and red lollipops were her favourite of favourites.

And that is what she was doing, sucking a red lollipop, when the principal stormed out of the building, her green hair waving in the breeze, and came over to stand indignantly in front of Jenny.

The principal looked down at Jenny, her mouth wide open in astonishment.

"I can't believe my eyes," she said at last. "I never thought I'd see the day when a teacher – a teacher, mind you – would be sitting out in the school garden s lollipop!"

Jenny took the lollipop out of her mouth and was about to say how sorry she was. But she had no chance to say anything, as just at that moment the school secretary came running across the grass.

"There's a telephone call for you," she said to the principal. "And it's urgent."

The principal gave Jenny a withering

look, and turned on her heels. Then, together with the school secretary, she strode off in the direction of the office.

The telephone call turned out to be a very strange conversation indeed.

"I'm so sorry about not being there today," said a voice at the other end of the line. "I seem to have put the wrong day in my diary. I thought I was starting tomorrow."

Miss Ice frowned in annoyance.

"I have no idea what you're talking about," she snapped at the caller. "Where are you? And why do you think you should be here, rather than there? And *who* are you, anyway?"

"I was meant to be there today," said the voice. "I thought today was tomorrow. I mean I thought that tomorrow was today. I thought that . . ."

"But why do you think you have to be here tomorrow, or today?" said the principal in a voice that was by now becoming extremely vexed.

"Because I told you that I was going to be here, or rather there, today. I mean, that today was when I was going to start, rather than tomorrow."

The principal drew in her breath.

"Let's start at the beginning," she said coldly. "Who are you?"

"I'm your new teacher, of course," said

the voice. "I was meant to be starting today."

"But you have," said Miss Ice. "You're here."

"No I'm not," said the voice. "I'm not there. I'm here. And that's the problem."

"But I've just seen the new teacher," protested Miss Ice. "I've just been talking to her. She was sucking a lollipop . . ."

"A lollipop?" asked the voice at the other end, sounding very surprised. "I don't eat lollipops. I used to, of course, but that was a long time ago. Chocolates, yes, that's a different matter . . ."

Miss Ice cut her short. It was now

becoming clear to her that something very strange was happening.

"Very well," she said in her steeliest voice. "Very well. You don't eat lollipops and you're not here. Just come along as soon as you can."

And with that she put down the receiver and stormed out of the office.

Jenny was still sitting with her friends when Miss Ice returned. They had not noticed the principal return and they all got a shock when they heard the angry voice bellowing out behind them.

"Now I know," cried the principal, her voice cracking with anger. "You're not a teacher at all!" She paused. "You're a . . . you're a girl!"

Jenny dropped her lollipop. She could not deny it. It was all over.

"It wasn't my fault," she said. "I didn't want to be a teacher at all. I didn't start it . . ."

The principal, who was now quivering with rage, took a step forward, and stood on the lollipop. She looked down at her right shoe, which now had a lollipop stuck to it. Then she bent down to scrape off the sticky mess, and that was Jenny's chance.

"Run!" whispered Lucy. "Quick!"

Jenny leapt to her feet and ran across

the garden towards the school gate. The principal started to give chase, but Jenny was far too quick for her and had soon disappeared round the corner. She had made it!

After a while, Jenny stopped running and began to walk. She looked over her shoulder to see whether she was still being chased, but there was no sign of anybody following her. She breathed a sigh of relief and turned the corner into her own street.

As she did so, she almost bumped into a woman who was walking in the opposite direction.

"I'm sorry," said the woman, looking anxiously at her watch. "I wasn't really looking where I was going." She paused. "Could you help me? I'm very late, and very lost."

"Of course," said Jenny. "Where are you going?"

"Well," said the woman. "It's rather a long story. I put the wrong date in my diary. I thought today was tomorrow, or the other way round, I'm not sure. I'm trying to find the school near here. Street Pond School. I'm the new teacher there and I'm terribly late. I've just been speaking to the principal on the telephone — Miss Frost I think she's called — and she sounded terribly hot, I mean cold, about it all."

Jenny listened to this carefully, and as she did so she began to smile. This was the real teacher, the teacher whose place she had taken for the day.

"You're not far away," she said. "If you walk down that road, turn left, and then carry on all the way up the street you'll reach the school."

"Thank you," said the woman gratefully. "I do hope that my class has been looked after this morning."

"Oh I think they had quite an interesting morning," Jenny said. "They studied rats, I mean maths. And then they did gym. I shouldn't worry about that if I were you."

The real teacher thanked her and went off on her way. Jenny watched her as she went, pleased that they had bumped into one another. She liked the sound of the new teacher and she was sure that the pupils would too.

But Jenny had not yet solved all her problems. Although she had managed to get away from the school, she would have to go back there the next day. And what would happen then? How could you go back to a school where you had dyed the principal's hair green? Miss Ice would not forget something like that in a hurry.

Jenny was thinking of this, feeling quite miserable, as she walked in the front door of her house. So she paid very little attention to her mother's calling her until her mother rushed out of the sitting room and gave her a big hug.

"There you are!" her mother said. "What a relief! I've been so worried about you! Where were you?"

"At school," said Jenny simply.

"But the school telephoned," said her mother. "They said that you hadn't arrived this morning. You can imagine how worried I was!"

Jenny sat down and sunk her head in her hands. It was going to be very difficult to explain.

"I *was* at school," she said. "Or rather, I went to school. But there was an awful mistake, you see. They thought I was a teacher."

Her mother looked at her in astonishment.

"Do you mean they put you in charge of a class?" she exclaimed.

Jenny nodded.

"It was terrible to start with," she said. "But then it got better. In fact, I think that all the children enjoyed themselves very much."

"I see," said her mother. "Well, I shall be able to phone Mr Brown now and tell him not to worry."

Jenny was puzzled.

"Mr Brown?"

"The principal of Pond Street School," said her mother. "I spoke to him on the phone this morning. He was very puzzled as to why you weren't there."

"But the principal isn't Mr Brown," protested Jenny. "It's Miss Ice. She's a lady with green . . . I mean, red hair."

Jenny's mother looked surprised. Then a smile spread slowly over her face as she realised what had happened.

"Jenny," she explained, her voice

breaking into a laugh. "You went to Street Pond School, didn't you? That's the other school! You were due to go to Pond Street School."

Jenny began to laugh too.

"So I don't have to go back there," she said. "What a relief!"

She was very pleased that she would not have to face the principal again. She was also pleased that she would not have to explain to all her pupils at the school that she may have started off as a teacher but was coming back as a girl. That would have seemed very odd to everybody.

So she went to school the next day – to

the right school this time – and she was very happy there. She didn't have to sit at the teacher's desk and she did not have to conduct any lessons. It was wonderful to be able to sit there, not having to know the answers to everything.

And as for Street Pond School, well, her day there had changed things in more ways than one. A few weeks later, while she was helping her mother with her shopping, she met Alison, the friendly teacher, in the supermarket.

"There you are!" exclaimed Alison. "I'm really glad that I saw you. I wanted to thank you for making things so much better at the school."

Jenny was puzzled, but Alison explained everything to her.

"You see, after what happened in the staff room, we all decided that we would stand up to Miss Ice and not let her push us around quite so much. So we started to vote on all the important things. And since there were far more of us than of the principal, the school began to be run the way we had always wanted."

"I'm glad," said Jenny. "I thought that I had just caused trouble that day."

"Not at all," said Alison, smiling. "And another thing — Miss Ice got used to the new way of doing things and became far, far less bossy. She's really quite nice now!"

"I'm very pleased," said Jenny.

"But the oddest thing of all," said the teacher, "is what happened about Miss Ice's hair. She decided that she rather liked her hair the colour you made it — green. So now she has it dyed green permanently, and it suits her very well!"

"So everybody's happy?" asked Jenny.

"Yes," said the teacher. "Everybody is very happy. What's more, any time you'd like to come back as a teacher for a day or so, please do!"

Jenny thanked her warmly. She did not think that she would go back, but it was nice to know that the invitation was there. She thought back on her day as a teacher.

She hadn't done so badly after all. She had sorted out George Apple, and saved his life as well. She had stood up to Miss Ice, and made her much better while she was about it. And she had given the whole class something to laugh about. Perhaps she would go back now and then, just to make sure that things were still going well. *After all*, she thought, *I was really quite good at it*!

Ladies and gentlemen, boys and girls,
step right up for an amazing circus story
by Alexander McCall Smith . . .

Freddie Mole is an ordinary boy who gets a
cleaning job at the circus. He can't believe his luck
when he is asked to understudy some of the acts.
But can he really tame four growling lions?

Out now